Grind

Eric Walters

orca soundings

ORCA BOOK PUBLISHERS

Library and Archives Canada Cataloguing in Publication

Walters, Eric, 1957-
Grind / Eric Walters.

(Orca soundings)
ISBN 1-55143-586-1 (bound).-- ISBN 1-55143-317-6 (pbk.)

I. Title. II. Series.

PS8595.A598G75 2004   jC813'.54   C2004-904735-3

Summary: When Wally is badly injured skateboarding, Phillip must decide
what is more important—skating or making things right with his friends.

First published in the United States, 2004
Library of Congress Control Number: 2004110961

Orca Book Publishers gratefully acknowledges the support for its publishing
programs provided by the following agencies: the government of Canada
through the Book Publishing Industry Development Program, the Canada
Council for the Arts, the government of British Columbia and the
British Columbia Arts Council.

Cover design: Lynn O'Rourke
Cover photography: Eyewire

Orca Book Publishers
PO Box 5626, Stn. B.
Victoria, BC Canada
V8R 6S4

Orca Book Publishers
PO Box 468
Custer, WA USA
98240-0468

www.orcabook.com

08 07 06 • 5 4 3

Printed and bound in Canada.

*For all those who have the guts
to go big instead of going home!*

Chapter One

The bell rang, marking the end of both the school day and my nap. I reached down and grabbed my backpack, stuffed in my notebook and got out of my seat. Despite the slow start, I was still the first person through the door. That was the fastest either my mind or my body had moved all day.

The door closed behind me, cutting off the teacher yelling out his reminder about the test tomorrow. Didn't he understand that the school day was over? He should stop talking because I'd stopped listening. I knew there was a test and I'd definitely study for it. My plans were to cut first class and get ready for the test. For now, though, I was free.

I worked my way down the hall, weaving in and out of the crush of kids moving in the other direction. I didn't know most of them, but what I did know was that we all wanted the same thing—to get out of the building. I reached my locker, opened it up and threw in the backpack. There was nothing in there that I was going to need tonight. The only thing I needed was in the bottom of my locker and—

"Hey, Phil!"

I turned around. "How's it going, Wally?"

"School's over, so it must be good. What do you want to do?"

"I figured I'd go straight home. I have some chores to do around the house. Then I'll finish all my homework and do some *extra* math, just so I can be better prepared. Then

I'll read a little bit from the Bible before I turn in for the night because early to bed, early to rise makes you healthy, wealthy and wise."

"Seriously," Wally asked.

"Ask a stupid question, get a stupid answer. What do you think I'm going to do?" I reached down into my locker and grabbed my skateboard.

"I knew we were going skating," Wally said, his board tucked under his arm. "I just wanted to know *where*."

"I was thinking behind the Super Save."

"That's good for me. I don't imagine Lisa will be coming."

I turned around, slammed the locker closed and clicked on the lock. "What do you think?"

"Still a little sensitive, huh?"

"Not sensitive. Just tired of people asking me. You want to skate or what?" I demanded.

Wally took his board out from under his arm and held it out. "I'm not carrying this just to look cool."

"That's good, because that whole cool thing just isn't working for you," I joked.

The crowd was already starting to thin out. That meant some people had escaped before me. I didn't like that. We hurried down the corridor. I thought about how much faster we could move if we just put down the boards and jumped on. Of course, that would have meant a suspension.

Outside the school, the parking lot was a crush of cars, backing out of spots, bumping along the rows, lined up ready to leave. Kids snaked between the cars. We worked our way through the traffic. Again, skating would have been faster, but the same rules applied in the parking lot — get caught skating and you got suspended. It felt like there were more rules and punishments applied to skateboarding than there were to selling drugs.

We finally reached the edge of the parking lot. Just a few feet short of school property I put down my board, jumped on and pumped my way to freedom.

The path was smooth, sloping down, leading to a tunnel that went under the main road.

There were clumps of people along the path ahead of us. I liked that. People became pylons to skate around. I pumped harder, picking up more speed. I zipped in and out, avoiding people, but trying to *just* avoid them.

I bent down low, allowing the hill to work for me, picking up speed. Just at the bottom of the hill there was a set of stairs — twelve of them. The stairs got closer and closer. I flew off the top, getting great air, grabbing the board with one hand, flying, hitting the pavement with a bump and then flying forward off the board and face planting in the grass and gravel at the side of the path.

I heard the screams and laughs from behind me — people on the path. I picked myself up.

"You okay?" Wally asked. Board in hand, he'd run down the stairs.

I spit out bits of grass and grit. "I'm good."

"You didn't hurt your wrist?" he asked.

"I made sure I landed on my face." I'd just got the cast off three days before. I'd broken it boarding.

"Nice move," said a big guy walking by with a couple of giggling girls. He was in grade twelve and played football.

"Like you could do better."

He stopped. "What did you say?" he demanded.

"I just said thanks."

"Let's keep it that way," he snarled and started to walk away again.

"Doing that jump is dangerous enough by itself without you trying to pick a fight with a guy big enough to eat you for lunch," Wally said.

"I'm not afraid of him."

"If you're not afraid of him then you're even more stupider than I thought."

"More stupider? Who taught you how to speak?"

"Actually you did. You and television."

"A dynamite combination."

I'd first met Wally in grade four. He was the new kid — straight off the plane from Poland —and I was asked by the teacher to be his buddy. The only English words he knew were Nike, Coke and hello. We'd been friends ever since.

"Don't you ever get tired of missing that jump?" Wally asked.

"I was tired of *missing* it the first time. That doesn't mean that I'm gonna stop trying. I'm not going to let a few misses discourage me."

"A *few*?" Wally scoffed. "This is May. You first tried that jump in February."

"February 10."

"Okay, February 10. And every day on the way home from school you've tried it. That's got to be at least sixty times."

"It's not that many!" I protested.

"Twenty times a month for three months. You do the math."

"Whatever. But this time was the closest ever, don't you think?"

"Not bad. Did you ever think if you took it with a little less speed you'd get a little less air and you just might make it."

"Go big or go home," I said.

"That's a great bumper sticker, but with you it's often *Go big and then go to the hospital*."

"Funny."

"I wasn't trying to be funny."

"I don't get hurt that often," I argued. I deliberately tucked my right leg behind my left to hide the place where I'd just ripped the knee of my jeans. And the knee *underneath* the jeans.

"That's just wrong," Wally said. "Thanks to you I feel like I'm on a first-name basis with every ambulance driver and emergency department nurse in the city."

"It's not that bad."

"They practically stop me on the street and say, 'Hey Wally, how's Phillip doing?'"

"It's not like you've never been hurt," I said.

"A broken arm and a concussion and some scrapes and cuts. That doesn't even put me in the same league as you."

There was no point in arguing—he was right. I'd broken both wrists—at different times—my collarbone, three fingers, sprained my ankle three or four times, dislocated my knee, had three concussions and more scrapes and cuts than I could count. And of course that didn't include my two front teeth—or more accurately my two capped teeth that replaced the ones I'd broken off. I was board sliding a rail when my board slipped and I hit the rail face first, snapping the teeth off right above the gum line. It was eerie to feel two little Chiclets floating around in my mouth—and then realize I wasn't chewing gum.

Actually I'd been injured so often that the hospital thought I was being abused. They'd even sent a social worker to the house to talk to my parents. I'd never seen my father that angry—so angry that he looked like he *could* beat somebody up. I finally convinced the social worker that I wasn't trying to "hide anything" but just got hurt skating.

"All I'm saying," Wally continued, "is that if you took it down a notch or two, you'd make the jumps and save the injuries."

"I always make the *jumps*," I argued.

"What are you talking about?"

"I make the jumps. It's the landings that I'm having trouble with."

Chapter Two

We skated across the store's parking lot, keeping one eye out for traffic and the other for security. If security drove up, that would be the end of this skate session.

We skated to the back of the store. There was a big truck backed up and pressed tight to the delivery door. It was still early and no other skaters were around yet.

We warmed up by skating a couple of low ledges. I was always anxious to skip the easy stuff, but I knew if I didn't warm up a little, the big tricks were impossible.

"Ready for some excitement?" I asked Wally.

"Ready enough."

I rolled up the bank lining the back wall of the store, gaining speed as I started down. I ollied up to the hand rail, 50/50ing down it and hitting the pavement...staying on my wheels and on my feet. Nice. Very nice.

I leaped off the board, kicked it at the end and it jumped into the air. I caught it and tucked the board under my arm. I watched as Wally was about to hit the bank. He gained speed as he came down and ollied up and onto the rail — it was a ten set — doing a board slide. He almost landed it but bailed at the very end, the board shooting in one direction while he ran in another. I leaned down and grabbed the board as it tried to skitter by me.

"Almost stuck it," I said as I handed him the board.

"Almost," he answered. "Feels strange to be here."

"Why? We're here all the time."

"Strange to be here without Lisa."

"You still going on about that?"

"I know. It's just strange not to have her around. Mind if I ask you a question?"

"Would you stop if I said no?"

He shook his head. "Do you think you two will get back together?"

I shook my head. "She's still pretty mad."

"Do you blame her?" Wally asked.

I shrugged. "Maybe it was for the best. We were starting to drift apart."

"Drift apart? That sounds like something you'd hear on a soap opera. What exactly does that mean?"

"It means we just don't have that much in common."

"You live to board, and she's the best female skater I know."

"But that's not enough," I said.

"Well, how about the fact that she's one of the hottest girls in our grade."

"She's okay."

"Okay? Lisa's a lot more than just okay."

"I've known her a lot longer than you have, and there are things you don't know about her."

"Things like what?"

"For one thing, she likes to be in charge and tell people what to do."

"Then there's another thing the two of you have in common."

"You are just such a funny, funny guy. A better question than why I'm *not* with Lisa anymore is why I *am* with you."

"Who else would put up with you?" he asked.

"Shut up and skate," I said. "I want to see you land it."

"Land what?" Wally asked.

"Don't you be the one acting stupid now. You know what I want to see."

"I know," he said, shaking his head. "I just wish I *could* land it."

We were talking about a trick Wally had been working on. It was a heel flip onto the railing and then a front sideboard slide down. Wally had been trying it for weeks and just missing. I knew he could land it if he just kept trying.

"Come on, today's the day. I can feel it," I said.

"The way you can feel the pain in your knee," he said, gesturing to the rip in my pants. I hadn't noticed up to that point that the tear was now blood-stained.

"Just try. Don't wimp out. Go on."

Wally reluctantly nodded.

I wasn't trying to be mean. He was so close. I knew he could do it. That was the problem. I knew it, but he didn't. Every time, he'd bail out because he didn't believe he could land it. That was what was wrong with Wally's skating. He had great feet — probably better than mine — but he'd bail out, jump off his board, when it started to look bad. And with the hard moves it almost always looked bad.

Wally came off the bank, loaded with speed, milking the transition. He popped his board and it landed a perfect 50/50 on the rail! It was a perfect grind, and then he kicked off and the board spun around and…he jumped off, landing on his feet.

Part of me felt like cheering, part felt like

booing and the rest felt like crying. He could be so good if he let himself.

"Nice, Wally. You want to try it again?"

"Maybe tomorrow."

"Why not now? We have all night."

"Not me. I've got about an hour before I go."

"What's the rush?"

"Math test, remember?"

Wally and I were in different classes, but we had the same math teacher and the same test coming up tomorrow.

"Just because you don't need to study doesn't mean I don't."

"I'm going to study," I said.

"But probably no more than a few minutes."

"That's all you need to do if you want to pass," I said. "Passing would be perfect."

"Perfect is a hundred last time I checked," Wally said. "If you studied more, you'd do more than just pass."

"If I studied more I wouldn't have as much time for skating or — "

I stopped mid-sentence as I saw the car glide around the corner. Wally turned around and saw it too. The car came to a stop at the corner. There were two people in the front.

"You think it's security?" Wally asked.

"Not in a car that fancy."

"Then what are they doing?"

"How would I know?" I asked. "Maybe it's something innocent…like a drug deal. Let's just skate," I said and shrugged.

I put a foot onto my board and pushed off to get up speed. I went partway up the bank, rocked, and reverted as I came back down. I left the transition, kicked the tail of the board, flipping with my foot at the same time so it flew up into the air, landing again, with me on top! It was a hard flip — a little wobbly, but I stayed on the board.

"Nice move!" Wally cheered.

I shot him a smile and started pumping again, building up my speed. I wanted to try the railing and—

"They're getting out of the car," Wally said.

I flipped the board up and caught it,

spinning around to look. One guy, the driver, had gone to the back and was leaning into the open truck. The other guy was standing beside the car. In his hands was a camera — a video camera.

"Why would he have a camera?" Wally asked.

I shook my head.

"Do you think they could be security?"

"Why would security have a camera?"

"I heard that in some places they're taping kids so they can prove they warned them to leave, and if they come back they can have them charged with trespassing," Wally explained.

"That's just bizarre."

"It may be bizarre, but it's true. We better get out of here."

I didn't want to leave, but Wally might be right. It was then that I noticed the second guy. He slammed the trunk closed. On his head was a helmet. Tucked under his arm was a board. They weren't security. They were here to skate and tape!

Chapter Three

Both guys were older than us — maybe eighteen or twenty. The one guy climbed onto his board. He did a couple of powerful pumps with his right leg, and the board practically jumped forward. Then, out of the blue, he popped the board into the air, spinning a 360 flip and landing back on top of it! Perfect! He wasn't just a skater, he was a very good skater.

The other guy — the one with the camera — ran behind him, lens to his eye, capturing what the skater was doing.

He rolled up the asphalt bank and came back down fakie, hit the flat and kick flipped the board. Another trick hit with no effort. He skidded to a stop right in front of us, kicking the board up and catching it in the air.

"How's it going?" he asked.

"Good," I said. I didn't know who he was, so I wasn't going to give much away. Being a good skater didn't mean he was necessarily a good guy.

"And for you?" he asked Wally.

Wally didn't answer. I looked over at him. He was wide-eyed and open-mouthed. He looked stunned.

"It's going good…really good…Mr. Bam Bam."

"Actually, Bam Bam will do," the man said.

"You know him?" I asked Wally.

Wally still looked stunned, but he squeezed out some words. "Of course I know him. *You* know him."

"I don't know any…" I stopped mid-sentence as the man took off his helmet to reveal a wild thatch of bleached blond hair. I did know him. It was — *he* was — Bam Bam Bradley. I knew him from articles and pictures in *Thrasher* and *Transworld Skateboarding* and skating videos. He was a professional skater! Suddenly I felt as stunned as Wally looked.

"You really are him … Bam Bam."

"That's my name," he chuckled.

It wasn't his real name — that was Brian. He got the nickname Bam Bam because he looked like Fred Flintstone's neighbor's kid who was named Bam Bam. And for the fact that he was famous for destroying his board — pounding it into the pavement or smashing it against a rail — when a trick didn't go the way he wanted. Bam, bam, bam, and that was the end of his board.

"What are you doing here?" Wally sputtered. That was a good question.

Bam Bam held out his board. "I've come to skate, if that's okay with you two."

"Of course it's okay," I exclaimed.

"It would be, like, our *honor* to skate with you," Wally gushed.

"That's cool," Bam Bam said, "although I hope you'll understand I don't really have a lot of time, so I was thinking maybe I could skate and you two could watch while we film."

"We could do that," Wally said.

"Sure, it'll be like watching our own video except it will be live," I added.

"And in living color," Bam Bam said.

"I was just wondering," Wally asked, "how do you know about this spot?"

"I heard about it in a skating chat room on the net."

"You go into chat rooms?" Wally asked. "I go into chat rooms all the time. Maybe we've talked."

"Probably not. I used to talk, but now I just listen in. When I used to say it was me, people didn't believe me. They burned me for being a poser."

I chuckled. Imagine talking to Bam Bam but not knowing it.

"Either of you ever visit my web site?" Bam Bam asked.

"I have," Wally said.

"I'd like it if people visited it every day. The more hits, the more I get paid."

"You have to pay to go on your web site?" I asked.

"Not you. The sponsors. You know those ads at the top and bottom of the page and the pop-ups?"

I nodded. I didn't know about his site, but there were ads on almost every site.

"Those people pay me money in exchange for me putting their ad on my site. The more people who visit—the more hits—the more they pay me."

"I'll go there every day... a few times a day if you want!" Wally offered enthusiastically.

"That's what I like to hear."

"Speaking of web sites," his camera guy said, "what would you two think about being on Bam Bam's site?"

"You want *us* on his site?" Wally asked. He sounded as astonished as I felt.

"What trick do you want us to do?" I questioned.

"Not a trick," the camera guy said.

"Yeah, I'm the only one who skates on my web page," Bam Bam said.

"Then what do you want?" I asked.

"I shot the two of you reacting when you met Bam Bam," the camera guy said.

Unless my expression was different than Wally's, he wanted shots of us looking like a couple of idiots.

"That would be incredible!" Wally exclaimed. "Incredible!" He paused. "How much do we have to pay you to be on the page?"

Both the camera guy and Bam Bam burst into laughter.

"You don't have to pay anything," Bam Bam said.

"But I thought that people had to pay to be on your page," Wally said, sounding confused.

"Sponsors do. You two aren't sponsors. All I need is your permission, in writing, to put your photos up."

"You got it! Just show me where to sign!" Wally said excitedly.

The camera guy whipped out a couple of pieces of paper from his camera bag. "First I need to get your names."

"I'm Wally ... Walter Waltniski."

"Wow, your parents thought the name was so nice that they named you twice," Bam Bam joked. "Just like me."

The camera guy asked Wally how to spell his name and then wrote it down and held out the form. Wally signed it without looking. He could have been signing away his soul.

"And you?" the camera guy asked.

"I'm Phillip Falcone."

"Falcone? How do you spell that?"

"Like the bird, Falcon, with an extra e at the end."

"Falcon," Bam Bam said. "That is so cool. Just like Tony Hawk, except isn't a falcon stronger?"

"I don't know about stronger, but a falcon is the fastest thing in the world," I said.

"Cool. Now if you two don't mind, I've got to get to work. We need to keep updating our web site. If people know there's new material they're more likely to visit every day... just like Wally here is going to do from now on."

Bam Bam skated off while his camera guy finished getting my signature — at least I read the form — and then moved into position to start filming. Wally and I stood off to the side.

"Wonder what he's going to do?" Wally asked.

"He does so many tricks, it could be anything."

"Whatever it is, I know it's going to be good," Wally said. "He's just about the best."

Almost on cue, Bam Bam pumped to gain enough power to climb the bank. He did another revert — perfect like all the rest — charged down the hill and ollied up and onto the rail. He tail slid along the rail and then he kicked it out, landing heavily on his side, the board flying off, skittering across the pavement toward us. I bent down and grabbed the board as it rolled by.

"Do you think he's hurt?" Wally asked.

"It's not him that's going to get hurt," I said.

"What do you mean?"

I held up the board. "Bam, bam, bam."

Bam Bam slowly got to his feet. He had a scowl on his face as he came walking toward us. I looked at his board. It was beautiful, almost new, hardly a scuff mark on it, expensive trucks and wheels.

"Board," he said.

Reluctantly I held it out toward him. I had to fight the insane urge to tell him he couldn't have it. Better he bam bam the board than me. I handed it to him and braced myself for the explosion that I *knew* was going to follow.

"Thanks," Bam Bam said. He turned and started back for the bank.

"Wait!" Wally called out, and Bam Bam turned around. "Aren't you going to…going to…you know…break the board?"

Bam Bam smiled and shook his head. "I don't really beat up boards, especially ones I like."

"But I've seen the videos," Wally said.

"That's different. That's part of my gimmick, part of my image."

"Your image?" I questioned. "I thought you did it because you hated missing a trick."

"I do hate missing a trick, but if I broke up a board every time I missed a trick, I'd run out of boards *and* money."

"You don't miss that much," Wally said. "I watch the videos."

Both Bam Bam and his camera guy burst out laughing again.

"Man, if we showed you all the misses, you'd be watching a ten-hour video," Bam Bam said. "We only show you the tricks we hit and a few misses that are most spectacular. It might take me an hour to land this trick I'm trying."

"You're joking, right?" Wally asked.

"No joke. If you stick around you'll see."

"But you're a pro," Wally protested. "I thought you were really *good*."

"I am a pro and I am really good. Nobody lands all their tricks. Tell me, what do you think is the most famous trick of all time?" Bam Bam asked.

I didn't even have to think about it. "Tony Hawk landing a nine."

"Yeah, the nine," Wally agreed.

The nine was a nine hundred-degree rotation — he turned two and a half times in mid-air, landing on the board and sticking the jump. He pulled it off at the X-Games, and it remained the best-known trick of all time.

"I have to agree," Bam Bam said. "Do you know how long it took him to land that trick?"

I shook my head.

"The shot you see on the videos, the one where he made it, was his *thirteenth* attempt that day."

"I didn't know," I said.

"And he'd been trying that trick, on a regular basis, for thirteen *years*," Bam Bam continued.

I gasped. "I had no idea."

"It isn't about the tricks you miss."

"Unless it's a spectacular miss," the camera guy said.

"Yeah," Bam Bam agreed. "What really count are the tricks you make."

"And capture on video," the camera guy said, holding up the camera. "And then you place them on your web site and videos."

"Yeah, the web site is the key. It's not the old-school days, when tournaments produced sponsors and money. Now it's all web- and Internet-related. Now any skater, especially if he has a gimmick, something different, can make a name for himself."

"Speaking of which," the camera guy said, "if we want to add to your name, we'd better get this trick on tape."

Bam Bam skated back up toward the bank. I knew that nobody made *every* trick, but somehow I just thought the pros made *most* of them. It made me realize that maybe they weren't that much different—or better—than me.

Chapter Four

Bam Bam leaned out of the window of the car and waved as they drove away. We both waved back. Wally jumped up and down like he was a little schoolgirl.

"Wasn't that amazing?" Wally gushed.

"Part of it was. Did you see how many times he missed that trick before he finally stuck the landing?"

Wally shrugged. "Man, I'm never going to wash this again." He held up his board, displaying the spot where Bam Bam had autographed it.

"Since when did you ever wash your board?"

"You know what I mean."

"All I know is that you were acting pretty goofy. He's just another skateboarder."

"A pro boarder, featured in videos, magazines and on the web. I'm going to check out the web as soon as I get home and see if they've put up our pictures."

"Great, something to look forward to. Do you think they're going to put the video of the trick on his page?"

"I guess. He sort of nailed it," Wally said.

"Sort of" was the best way to describe it. He stayed on his board for a few feet after landing before he bailed.

"I know it was a hard trick," I said, "but somehow I thought he would have got it sooner."

"I hate to admit it—especially after he signed my board—but he wasn't really that great," Wally said. "He wasn't that much better than you."

"Thanks…I guess."

"You know what I mean. I just thought because he was a pro he'd be fantastic."

"I guess the whole thing is to just do the same thing over and over again until you finally get it on video. Speaking of which, do you want to try your trick once more?"

"I'll pass on that for now. It's getting late and I have to go home and study for the math test."

"How about if we just stay a little bit—" I stopped as I saw the little white security car zoom around the corner of the grocery store. The car squealed to a stop, and the security guard jumped out and immediately started yelling at us.

Wally grabbed his backpack and his board, and I grabbed my board, and we started running. We cut across the grassy strip, through some beaten-up bushes and ducked through a hole in the chain-link fence. We stopped when we got safely through the hole. He never chased us very far. Actually, this particular guy was so chunky and out of shape that I didn't think he *could* chase us for long…or even fit through the hole in the fence.

"You better not come back!" he yelled, shaking his fist in the air.

"We won't come back!" I yelled as we leaned over the fence. "At least not until *tomorrow!*"

"You better hope I never catch you!" he hollered.

"You got no chance of catching us until you stop catching so many double bacon cheeseburgers!" I screamed back.

His face got all red and he began swearing and screaming and started waddling toward us. Wally ran away, but I stayed right by the fence, smiling and waving and laughing. Just before he reached the fence, I blew him a kiss and took off. He threw a series of new and exciting words in my direction, but there was no way he'd catch me.

Wally was waiting for me by the underpass.

"You really shouldn't try to tick him off," Wally said.

"He started being a jerk. I just gave it back to him. Stupid rent-a-cop."

"You heading home now?" Wally asked.

"In a while. I'm thinking I should go back to the Super Save and skate for a while longer."

Wally gave me a concerned look.

"Joking, just joking."

"You want to come to my place for dinner?"

"What are you having?" I asked.

"What does it matter? It'll be homemade, and good."

"Well…"

"Come on, my mother loves you coming for dinner. It gives her another chance to fatten you up. She thinks you're all skin and bones."

"I am, compared to your family." Wally was the oldest of five boys—five big boys. Two of Wally's little brothers were bigger than me, and it wasn't like I was small or anything.

"You sure there'll be enough?" I asked.

"There's always enough. Besides, you eat

like a bird so what does it matter?" Wally questioned.

"I eat. I just don't eat like you and your brothers." They could all eat their weight in homemade perogies.

"So, you coming or what?" he asked.

"I'm coming."

"Good, and try to eat more. You know how my mother is — if you don't eat enough she thinks you don't like her food, and if you don't like her food, you don't like her."

"In that case, she must think that you and your brothers really, *really* like her."

Chapter Five

"Your supper's on the table!" my mother yelled as I walked in the door.

Oops. I'd forgotten to call to tell her I was going to eat at Wally's. And when I started boarding home I met some people, and we started skating and I lost track of the time.

"But you're so late it's long since cold," she said as she appeared at the door.

"That's okay, I'm not really that hungry. I'm just going to head up to my room."

"We'd actually like you to join us at the table for a little conversation," my father said as he stepped through the doorway.

"What sort of conversation?" I asked. I knew this couldn't be good.

"Join us." My father walked toward the kitchen. My mother and I followed. We all sat down at the table.

"Where were you?" my father asked.

"Just skating."

"I assumed that. Why didn't you call?"

"I was skating and..." I shrugged.

"Maybe we didn't get any calls *from* you, but we certainly got a call *about* you," my mother said.

"What does that mean?" I asked.

"We got a call from that automated machine at your school telling us you were missing from first period."

"First period?" I asked, trying to sound innocent, knowing that I'd been in the donut shop during first period. "I was there," I lied.

"Were you?" my father asked.

"Who are you going to believe, your son—a human being—or some stupid machine?"

"A human being," my mother said. "We called the school back and spoke to a human being — the vice-principal — and he confirmed it."

I was going to say something about the vice-principal really not being that much of a human, but I thought better of it.

"I didn't miss *all* of it," I said, knowing that I was trapped. "I was just late."

"There was no reason for you to be late," my father said. "You know, it's time you started to take things more seriously."

"I take things seriously," I argued.

"We mean other than skating," my mother said.

"Skating is important."

My father laughed. "No, it's not. We think it's getting in the way of things, like school, that *are* important."

"It's not."

"If you spent as much time on school as you did on being on your board, then your marks would be higher," my mother said.

"And if you're not going to spend your time on school, maybe you should at least get a part-time job and earn some money," my father said.

I didn't answer. I didn't want a job. I just wanted to skate.

"It's time to get serious," my father repeated. "And serious things involve school or even working. Something that would either lead to a career or at least make you money. Do you understand?"

I nodded. I understood. That didn't mean I agreed.

"And we both understand that you must still be upset about breaking up with Lisa," my mother said.

"Why do people keep bringing that up?" I snapped. "It isn't like somebody died."

"You two were together a long time, and teenage relationships can be painful. We understand," she said.

I wanted to say something about it being so long since she'd been a teenager that I doubted she could remember that far back. I kept the words inside my head.

"If it's okay with you two, I'd like to go up to my room and study for my math test."

I sat in my room, in the dark, the only light coming from the computer screen. I jumped around from one web site to another. I'd found Bam Bam's site. I was relieved to see that no pictures of either Wally or me — looking stupid and stunned — were posted ... at least not yet.

I'd surfed from his site to a bunch of other skate sites. Lots of sites with a lot of different skaters doing a lot of different tricks.

It was funny. I'd seen a lot of these tricks before, but now I was thinking about them differently. I couldn't help but wonder how many times they'd missed it before they captured the one that worked on video. I knew if I had enough time, I could land a lot of those tricks myself.

On each site there were little ads and pop-ups. And now I understood how those ads worked. Every time I logged onto Bam Bam's web page — or anybody's web page — they were getting paid by those sponsors. Strange. Really strange.

And then — like a bolt of lightning — it came to me.

I picked up the phone and pushed the second button on my speed dial. It had just started to ring when it was picked up.

"Hello."

"Hey, Wally, what were you doing, sitting on the phone? I have an idea."

"How much potential pain and money is this going to involve?" Wally asked.

"It will involve a lot of money, but you're going to *make* it instead of *spend* it. And as for the pain, you know what they say, no pain, no gain."

"And how much pain is there going to be?"

"No more than usual."

"So, what's your idea?" Wally asked.

"I'll tell you tomorrow."

"Tomorrow?"

"Yeah, I'll meet you at the usual time in the cafeteria."

"If you aren't going to tell me now, then why did you call me?"

"Because it isn't just me and you who need to be at this meeting. This plan involves two other people, and I need you to get one of them to come."

"Who?" Wally asked.

"That guy in your computer science class. I don't know his name."

"That's helpful. There are fifteen guys in that class."

"He's the guy you were talking about, the guy's who's a real nerd, a techie, a genius."

"Nevin," Wally said.

"That's the name. Get him to be there."

"I can call him, but what am I supposed to tell him?"

"Haven't you been listening at all? We're going to meet in the caf at eight."

"I meant what do I tell him about why we're meeting?"

"You don't tell him anything. Just tell him to be there."

"I'll try," Wally said. "You said there were going to be two other people. Who's the second?"

"Lisa."

"Lisa? She's going to meet us tomorrow?"

"Why wouldn't she?"

"I can think of a few reasons," Wally said.

"You just get that Nevin guy to show up and I'll take care of Lisa. See you tomorrow, and don't be late."

"Me, late?" Wally exclaimed. "I'm the one who's always on time."

I hung up and chuckled to myself. Knowing Wally, he'd be there fifteen minutes early and anxious. Now for the hard part. I picked up the phone and pushed the first button on my speed dial. It rang and rang and rang. Maybe she wasn't home. Maybe she was out. Maybe she was out with somebody else.

"Hello." It was Lisa. "Hello?"

For a split second I thought about hanging up.

"Hi, Lisa…it's me."

Chapter Six

"It doesn't look like she's going to show," Wally said.

I looked up at the clock at the end of the cafeteria. It was almost a quarter after. Maybe he was right. She hadn't told me she wasn't going to come, but she hadn't said yes either.

"I've got to go soon," Nevin said.

"We have plenty of time until first bell, and even if you are late it's no big deal."

"Why don't you just tell us a bit of the plan while we're waiting?" Wally suggested.

"I'd rather wait until—" I stopped as I saw Lisa enter the cafeteria. "Here she is," I said. I watched her walk across the room. I noticed other guys watching her as well, turning their heads to follow her as she passed. I really was an idiot.

"Hey, Lisa, this is Nevin," Wally said.

She smiled and nodded. He looked down at the table like he was embarrassed to be around her.

"Let's hear it. You've got two minutes," Lisa said. She sat down and folded her arms across her chest.

I felt the hairs on the back of my neck bristle. I had the urge to just sit there and wait her out, not say a word for two minutes, but I thought she'd just get up and leave. I knew her well enough to know when she said two minutes, that's how long I had. She had to be in charge, just like me.

I took a deep breath. "Here's my plan. The three of us are the best skaters in the entire school, maybe in the entire area."

"You brought us here to say that?" Lisa questioned.

I ignored her. "And we can make money, lots of money, because we are such good skaters."

"I think I've heard enough," Lisa said and started to get up.

"You promised me two minutes," I said.

"Gee, I wouldn't want to break a promise or a commitment!" she snapped, glaring at me angrily.

"Come on, Lisa, just listen for another minute," Wally said. "Aren't you curious? I am."

"You mean you don't know what he's going to say either?"

Wally shook his head.

"You said Wally was in. That was one of the only reasons I agreed to come here this morning."

"I didn't say that!" I protested. I certainly had *implied* it, but I never *said* it. "Besides, he will be in as soon as he hears my plan."

Her face softened, her shoulders relaxed

and she slid back down into her seat. "Fine. You have one minute left."

"In the old days, skaters didn't make money, they just skated. Then there were contests and the prize money started small and got bigger. The best skaters also got sponsored to ride certain boards or trucks or wheels, or wear the right clothes. Then videos started and the money was even bigger. And now the way to make money, lots and lots of money, is to video tricks and have a web site."

"Thanks for the history lesson," Lisa said.

"Don't you see?" I asked.

"No."

"Me neither," Wally said.

"I do," Nevin said. Everybody looked at him. "You want to create your own web page, fill it with things other skaters want to see and then have pop-up and standard ads on the page to generate money."

"Exactly! That's exactly what I want to do!" This Nevin guy really was smart. "Does everybody understand?"

"I understand completely," Lisa said.

"I understand that this is probably the stupid-est thing you've ever suggested." She started to stand up again.

"And just what's so stupid about it?" I barked.

"How about *everything*."

"Could you be a little more specific?"

"For starters, do you know how hard it is to create a web page?"

"It's easy," Nevin said, answering for me. "I've made lots."

"But it would still cost money to do that," she said.

"No, it wouldn't," Nevin disagreed. "Not a cent. I already have all the software, graphics and enough space to park a dozen more pages on the net."

"Well...we still have to get the stuff to put on the web," Lisa continued.

"We'll do our best tricks on video, have a few still pictures, put up information about the three of us," I said.

"Then we still need to get a video camera and..." Lisa stopped mid-sentence and looked at Nevin. "Well?"

"I have state-of-the-art digital camera and video equipment," he said.

I tried hard to keep a smirk off my face. "Any other questions?"

Lisa didn't say anything, but I knew she was thinking it through some more. If there was some fault, she'd find it and bail. She really didn't want to be involved with me right now.

"And there's money to be made doing this?" she asked.

"Big money," I said.

She turned to Nevin. "Is he telling the truth?"

"Of course I'm telling the truth!" I protested.

"Excuse me for doubting your word." She turned back to Nevin. "Well?"

He nodded. "Lots of money if the site has things people want to see and there are sponsors."

"Do you have sponsors?" she asked me.

"No, not yet."

"Then how are we supposed to make money?" she demanded.

"If we have a site and enough people go on it, then we can attract sponsors. That's the way it works."

Nevin nodded in agreement, and she didn't argue.

"And just how will all this money be split?" Lisa asked.

"We'd all have a share," I said.

"Since there's four of us, I guess that share is twenty-five percent each," Lisa suggested.

"I was thinking that since it was my idea, and I am the best skater, that I should get a bigger share."

"That is so typical of you!" Lisa exclaimed.

"But it *is* my idea."

"Tell you what. Now that we all know about the idea, how about the three of us, me and Nevin and Wally, do it without you, and we can get one third of the money each."

"You can't do that!"

"Of course we could. Wally and me can do the tricks, and Nevin here is the one who knows all the computer stuff. I don't know why we need you!" She paused. "I know I've certainly found out that *I* don't need you."

"That's not fair!" I protested.

"Lots of things aren't fair! I've learned that the hard way!"

"Come on, Lisa," Wally said. "He's right...this time."

Lisa stood up. "Split it into quarters or *I* split."

"So you're in?"

She nodded. "For twenty-five percent."

I nodded. A quarter of something was better than half of nothing.

"Then I'm in," she said.

"Me too," Wally agreed.

"I'd do it for nothing," Nevin said.

"You'll do it for a quarter share of the profits," Lisa barked. "So when do we start."

"How about right after school?" I asked.

"I have to go home and change. We'll meet at five behind the Super Save."

I wanted to protest. Who did she think she was, acting like she was the leader? "Sure," I agreed.

Lisa's lips curled into a little smirk. She turned and walked away. We all watched her cross the cafeteria and disappear out the door.

"She really must have liked you at one time," Nevin said.

"What?"

"She really must have liked you before."

"Why would you think that?" I asked. There was nothing she'd done that would make anybody think that she had ever liked me.

"For somebody to hate you that much she must have really cared for you, and then you did something bad."

I turned to Wally.

"Don't look at me!" he said, holding up his hands. "I didn't tell him anything. I told you the guy's a genius."

"We had a misunderstanding," I said to Nevin. "That's all. It's nothing."

"Sure…nothing," Nevin said, although it was obvious he didn't believe me either.

"If we're all done, we better get to class," Wally said.

"I'm not going to class," Nevin said.

I was really starting to like this guy.

"What are you going to do?" Wally asked.

"I'm going to spend the day in the computer lab researching skating web sites to see what works and what doesn't, and then I'll set up the framework for our site."

"They'll catch you if you cut the whole day and hang around," I said. I knew that from first-hand experience.

"You don't understand," Nevin said. "I won't be *cutting* classes. I'm *allowed* to spend my time that way if I want."

"You're allowed to cut classes?" I asked.

"Yeah. I'm so far ahead in everything that they let me do pretty much anything I want."

"Anything?" I asked.

He shrugged. "Anything. I'm not even supposed to be in this school."

"What school are you supposed to be in?" I asked.

"Homelands."

"But Homelands is a middle school."

"And I'm supposed to be in middle school... grade seven."

That would explain why he was so small and looked so young. "Then what are you doing in high school?" I asked.

"It's like people say. I'm really, *really* smart. I'll see you guys after school."

Chapter Seven

I tapped my foot against the board. I stopped myself. I was trying hard not to look as nervous as I actually felt. It was a quarter past five — fifteen minutes later than we'd agreed to meet. I was here on time. Wally was early. Nevin, equipped with a fancy, expensive, digital video camera and another digital still camera, had arrived right on the dot. He'd excitedly tried to explain all the features of the cameras, but I couldn't follow his techno-geek speak and just nodded as if I understood.

"She should be here by now," I said.

"She's not usually on time for things. Did you think that cheating on her would make her start arriving on time?" Wally asked.

"I didn't cheat on her!" I protested.

Wally looked shocked. "What would you call taking another girl to a movie and making out with her?"

"First off, I didn't *take* her to the movie. We just sort of met there."

"I believe that about as much as Lisa did," Wally said.

I ignored him. "And second, we didn't make out. We kissed a couple of times. And really, it was more like *she* kissed *me*."

"You poor baby. Did that mean old girl overpower you and get you in a liplock?"

I fought the urge to say that at least *I* could get a girl to kiss me. I was learning when it was smart to keep my mouth shut — a painful lesson that had taken a lot of years to figure out.

"Are we going to get started?" Wally asked.

"Soon, she'll be here soon."

"We can do this without Lisa. You and I are both better skaters than she is," Wally said.

"We're better skaters, but she's a better *girl* skater," I said. "Having a girl on the site might get us more hits from girls who are skaters and from guys who like seeing girl skaters."

"I guess that makes sense," Wally said. "I just thought that you might want her involved for another reason."

"What other reason?" I asked, trying to sound innocent.

"Like maybe if you could get her to spend some time with you, she might forget what happened," Wally said.

"How about if we just skate and stop talking?" I suggested.

"We can do that." Wally turned around. "Hey, Nevin, you ready?"

"Yeah…sure…I guess."

Nevin had worked to cram himself in the gap between the rail and the wall. He had his head and one hand — holding the digital camera — sticking up above the railing. The plan was for us to grind the railing and he'd duck down just before we got there. If he timed it right, he'd get some great shots. If he timed it wrong, he'd *take* a great shot — to the side of his head.

"You want to go first?" I asked.

"How about if Lisa goes first instead?"

He gestured behind me and I turned around. Lisa had just rolled around the corner and was skating toward us.

"You want to do something smart?" Wally said.

"What do you mean?"

"Just say hello and don't ask her why she's late."

"I wasn't going to do that," I said. Actually that was exactly what I was going to do. "I'm going to make my first run."

I dropped the board to the ground, put a foot on it and starting pumping. I needed enough speed to get up on the rail. This first run was going to set the tone for the whole day — for the whole project.

Closing in on the rail I looked up and saw Nevin, staring through the lens of the camera. I had to just hope he ducked in time. I ollied onto the rail and five-o'ed. I slid the length, hit the end and fell off the board, plowing into the pavement.

"Fantastic!" Nevin said. "That was fantastic!"

I pushed myself up onto my knees. The skin and scabs were torn and I was bleeding. What was a session without a little blood?

"That wasn't the way that trick was supposed to end, so it wasn't that fantastic."

"It doesn't matter how it ended. You have to see how it started. Here, have a look."

I walked over to Nevin. Wally and Lisa came over too. He rewound the scene.

"Here, look," Nevin said.

The screen showed me skating, then jumping up on the rail, grinding toward the camera at breakneck speed, getting bigger and bigger until the camera dropped and the board blotted everything out. Nevin was right. That was amazing!

"Let me go next," Wally said.

He skated over to take up position, and Nevin wedged himself back under the rail. Lisa and I retreated out of the way.

"Nice of you to show up," I said.

"I was thinking about not coming," she said, "but I didn't want to let *Wally* down. After all, he's never let me down."

I tried not to say anything. Having Lisa even angrier wasn't part of the plan.

"Why don't you skate the next run?" I suggested.

"Since you've already skated and now Wally is skating, I guess it would be my turn." She dropped her board to the ground, put a foot down and pushed herself away.

If part of my plan was to get her to talk to me, it really wasn't working out so far.

Chapter Eight

"We should call it soon," Wally said.

I had to agree. "Maybe make another run or two. There's not much light left anyway."

"Or memory," Nevin said. "I've shot a whole bunch of video and more than a hundred pictures."

"Do you still have some room left?"

"A few minutes."

"Then let's use it up and go home." I started to skate to the top of the slope.

A car came squealing around the corner.

"Security!" Wally screamed.

I did a quick flip turn and headed back toward Wally and Lisa, who were heading for the hole in the fence.

Just then, out of nowhere, another security car came spinning around the other corner, heading straight toward me. It was going to hit me!

The car slammed on its brakes and I leaped up into the air, landing on the hood of the stopped car! My momentum carried me forward and I ran up the windshield, over the roof, down the trunk and leaped to the ground just as my board, which had rolled under the car, came out from the back.

I jumped onto the board and kept going.

I got to the edge of the grass, grabbed my board and started for the hole in the fence.

Wally and Lisa were already waiting. They both looked shocked.

"That was incredible!" Wally xclaimed.

"You just gypsy hopped a security car!" Lisa yelled.

"Where's Nevin?" I turned around. He was still over by the wall, partially hidden behind some crates. I didn't think the security guards had noticed him because they were so focused on me. If they turned around and saw him, they had him trapped.

The guards — one in each car — had climbed out of their vehicles.

"Did you like that trick?" I yelled at them. "Come over here and I'll climb up and down the two of you!"

"What are you doing?" Lisa demanded.

"We have to have them look this way... *come* this way, so Niven can get away."

I popped back through the hole so I was on the same side of the fence as the guards.

"Come on you losers!" I yelled. "Come on over — or are you too scared?"

The two men started toward me. They were both big — one fat and the other just plain big. I looked past them to Nevin. He wasn't moving. Why wasn't he moving?

Was he too scared or—he was still taping! Unbelievable. He was either incredibly brave or incredibly stupid. Maybe both.

I backed away as the two guards closed in. Suddenly the big guy started to run. He moved incredibly fast for somebody his size.

I ducked back through the hole and started running. Wally and Lisa were already off. I looked behind me. The security guard hadn't stopped at the hole—he was still coming, still running after me! I dug down deeper and started to run as fast as my legs would carry me.

"Keep running!" I yelled to Wally and Lisa. I spied them waiting up ahead by the underpass. They started running again. I kept gaining until I finally caught up. At that point I risked a look over my shoulder. The path behind us was empty.

"What happened to Nevin ... did any-body see?" I asked, straining to catch my breath.

"He got away," Wally said. "He got up and ran just after you started back for the hole."

"Good, then we're all okay."

"I'll call him when I get home," Wally said, "just to make sure."

"That's very considerate," Lisa said, "but of course that's what I expect of *you*."

"Let's just go home," Wally said, jumping in before I could say anything.

I was getting tired of her comments, but what choice did I have?

"I'll see you two tomorrow," I said.

Wally and Lisa lived close together while my house was in the other direction. I watched them walk away. It was strange. It used to be me walking with Lisa.

Chapter Nine

The PA crackled to life. "Could Phillip Falcone please report to the computer lab."

The computer lab? The only times my name had ever been called over the PA were to get me to go to the office. This made no sense. I wasn't even *taking* computer science this term. Maybe the vice-principal was giving detentions there because there was space for more kids. Then again, what had I even done to deserve a detention?

I had a sense of dread. What if I just left? Nobody would even know if I'd heard the announcement or not. I could just leave...but I couldn't. My curiosity won out.

I opened the door to the computer lab. It looked to be deserted. Row upon row of machines sitting on tables and—

"Phil!" Wally yelled out.

He was standing, partially hunched over a computer. Sitting at the monitor was Nevin. Lisa was sitting beside him. I guessed I wasn't in trouble.

"We had them page you," Wally said. "You have to see this."

"Nevin finished the web site," Lisa said.

"A web site is never really finished," Nevin said. "It's a constantly growing and changing thing, almost like it's alive."

"It may not be finished, but it's perfect," Wally said.

"Not perfect, but good enough to park on the web," Nevin said. His fingers started to fly across the keyboard. "It is now on the web and anybody, anywhere in the entire world, can see it."

"How about somebody right here?" I asked. "Could I see it?"

"Sure." His fingers started dancing on the keys. Red flames filled the screen. The flames faded away and outlines of skaters shot across the page, accompanied by the sound of wheels rolling on pavement.

"Beautiful opening," Wally said.

The skateboards all started coming together, forming some sort of pattern — letters — they were making letters! Then the letters became words: HOGTOWN TRIO!

"What does that mean?" I asked.

"That's you three," Nevin explained. "My research showed that all the skating groups had a name. You know, like the Bones Brigade or Dogtown or Warped. I liked the sound of the Hogtown Trio."

"It sounds like a musical group," Lisa said.

"Like a polka band," I added.

"And what would be wrong with that?" Wally asked. "You got something against polka bands?"

"Wally, we know you're Polish and that you used to play the accordion, but still."

"We can change the name if you want," Nevin offered. "But first look at the rest of the site."

He scrolled down. There was a big box with birds, like hawks or eagles, flying around. The text said PHILLY FALCON.

"Philly Falcon?" I gasped. "You changed my name?"

"I wanted something more catchy. I thought Falcon seemed more exciting. What do you think?"

"I think a guy named Nevin shouldn't be picking on anybody else's name," I said.

"Nevin is a good name. Besides, it's not me who wants to be a skating star. I'm just the webmaster. Do you want me to click in and show your tricks?"

"No," Lisa said. "First let him see the whole page. Once he starts looking at himself he won't even realize there are two other people on the site."

Nevin scrolled down and there was a picture of Lisa in full skating gear.

"How come you get to keep your name?" I asked.

"Look again," she said, pointing at the screen.

"What? You're still Lisa and…" I looked harder. Lisa was spelled L I I S A.

"There's a typo," I said.

"No there isn't. I spelled it that way to make it different," Nevin said. "I wrote a line on Lisa's page that says, 'Whenever she skates she attracts eyes.' Clever, huh?"

"I'm not sure about that. It just looks like she can't spell or her parents stutter."

Lisa laughed. That sounded so good. It had been a long time since I'd made her laugh.

"Now show him mine," Wally suggested.

Nevin scrolled down some more. There was a picture of Wally that looked like he was completely upside down.

"When did you take that picture?" I asked.

"Yesterday. It looks like he's inverted because I tipped the camera," Nevin explained.

"Do you like my name?" Wally asked.

Big letters said Wally the Wall Waltniski.

"Not bad," I admitted.

"And there's still one more section you should look at before you look at the shots of you three skating," Nevin said.

He moved the mouse to scroll down to the bottom of the page. The final section was called SKATEBOARDING ISN'T A CRIME. He clicked the mouse and the screen faded and then opened up again. It was a shot of me skating. Then the security car came into view, skidded to a stop, and I leaped onto the hood and raced over the top of the car, jumping down off the back.

"I didn't know you'd filmed that!" I exclaimed.

"I kept going. But wait, watch, the best part is still to come!"

As I skated away, the door of the car popped open and the security guard jumped out and started to run—wait, the guard had a pig's head! And as he ran after me, little cartoon balloons came out of his mouth saying "oink," and the whole computer started making pig sounds!

Wally and Lisa and I all exploded into laughter.

"Nevin, you are a genius!" Wally yelled, slapping him on the back.

"This was nothing. I could teach a monkey how to do that. So, do you like it?"

"It's amazing," Lisa said.

"Can we go into our pages and look at the skating now?" I asked.

"Definitely," Nevin agreed. "And after that we only have two things to do."

"What two things?" I asked.

"The first one's easy," he said. "I'm going to register the site on all the major search engines so they can start directing people to our page."

"And the second thing?" I asked.

"This one is a little more time consuming, but it could be fun. We're going to go to a few dozen skater sites and chat rooms and talk to people about this incredible new web site we just saw — our web site." He paused. "Of course we're not going to use our names or tell them it's our web site."

"Nevin, that is really, truly, sneaky and devious," I said.

"Thank you," he said.

"That's some compliment," Lisa said, "when you consider that you're talking to a person who's an expert on sneaky and devious."

"So how do we get started?" Wally said, jumping in to break the tension.

"I've already set the lab computers up so they're connected to the different sites and chat rooms."

"Which computers?" I asked.

"All the computers," Nevin said, gesturing around the room.

"There have to be a hundred computers in here," I said.

"Eighty-seven that work, so that's how many I've connected."

"You want us to visit eighty-seven sites?" I questioned.

"No, I want you to visit one fourth of the sites. If you want to attract sponsors you have to get hits," Nevin said. "I've put a counter on the very bottom of our page."

He scrolled down again. There was a little wheel that read 1234 visitors.

"We've had that many visitors already?" I asked.

Nevin laughed. "Of course not. I just didn't want anybody to think that nobody had visited. Everybody wants to go to a site that's popular."

"Makes sense," Wally agreed.

"And I've added a place where they post comments and talk to us," Nevin said. "Sort of like an interactive guest book."

"Excellent. This looks like it could be fun. Let's hit the chat rooms and get some interest started," Wally said.

"First things first. Let's explore the site fully to see your tricks," Nevin said. "Then we'll start spreading the word…around the whole world."

Chapter Ten

"Phillip, get up."

I rolled over. It was my mother, standing in the doorway. It was dark.

"Wally's on the phone for you," she said.

"Wally? Why is he calling…what time is it?"

"It's six in the morning and I have no idea why he's calling so early. Pick up the phone and ask him yourself."

I rolled over and grabbed the phone from the night table. "Hello."

"Phil, have you seen it?" he asked excitedly.

"I was sleeping. All I've been seeing is the inside of my eyelids."

"The web site! You have to log on to our site!"

"I saw it yesterday. I don't think it's changed much overnight."

"Wanna bet? Just look at it."

"All right, but this better be good." I rolled out of bed, keeping the mobile phone in my hand and walking over to my desk. I tapped the computer and the screen came to life. Our web site was already on the screen. I'd left it there last night when I went to sleep.

"Looks the same to me," I said.

"Scroll down."

I moved down the page. It all looked the same.

"What is it I'm supposed to see?" I asked.

"The bottom. Look at the visitor count."

I could only imagine that Wally was so excited because a few people had looked at our site. I scrolled to the visitor counter and—"Oh my god…that can't be right." It read 11 924. "Nevin must have gone back in and set the numbers higher," I said.

"He didn't," Wally said. "I already talked to him this morning."

As I watched, amazed, shocked, the visitor count began flipping over, getting higher and higher as more people logged on.

"That can't be right," I said. "How could that many people be visiting our site, especially in the middle of the night?"

"But it *isn't* the middle of the night—it *wasn't* the middle of the night in Japan and China and Australia."

"What are you talking about?"

"Go to the guest book. We've had visitors from lots of different countries. They don't call it the World Wide Web for nothing."

I didn't know what to say. I was speechless.

"Phil, are you still there?" Wally asked.

"I'm here. Does Lisa know?"

"Not yet. I wanted to call you and then I figured you'd probably be the one who wanted to call her. Good luck."

"Thanks," I said.

"That's okay. That's what friends are for. And Phil, if you do eventually convince her to get back together with you, treat her good this time."

"I'll try," I said.

"You better do more than just try, because, I'm warning you, the next time you two break up, I don't care if you are my best friend, I'm giving it a shot myself."

"You're going to ask Lisa out?"

"Don't sound so shocked. She might go out with me you know."

"I wasn't shocked. I was just thinking."

"About?"

"That she probably deserves some-body better...I mean better than me," I explained.

"She probably does, but that doesn't mean you should give up yet."

"I'm not giving up. Giving up isn't some-thing I'm good at."

"That I know," Wally said. "Nevin wants us to meet before class," he added. "Can you be there at eight?"

"Considering I'm up an hour earlier than usual already, I think I can manage. I'll let Lisa know."

Chapter Eleven

We stood around the computer, staring at the screen. As we watched, the number of hits on the site kept growing. It was unbelievable.

"This goes way beyond anything I had ever imagined," I said.

"Didn't you imagine sponsors and making money?" Nevin asked.

"Yeah, I thought that could happen."

"This is the Internet. Anything that's going to happen will happen fast," Nevin said.

"We've already been approached by e-mail by a skateboard company."

"What company?" Wally asked.

"They're new. It's called Street Illegal Boards. They're sending us their product, new boards for everybody."

"The new boards...how much do we have to pay?" Wally asked.

"You don't pay anything. They give you the boards so that people can see you skating on their product."

"But I like my old board," Wally said.

"You can like it all you want, but if we want them to sponsor the web site we have to have shots of you three skating on their board."

"They want to sponsor our page?" I asked, not believing my ears.

"Just a small ad to start, and a link to their home page where people can order from them."

"And they'll pay us for this ad, right?" I asked.

"The standard fee. A penny a hit."

"A penny? That's nothing!" I scoffed.

Nevin looked confused. "Over ten thousand people visited the site last night. That works out to over one hundred and twenty five dollars."

"That can't be right," I said.

"Believe me, I'm hardly ever wrong when it comes to math," Nevin said. "We all made over thirty dollars while we slept. By the end of today that amount will double or triple."

"You mean I could make a hundred bucks today?" Wally asked.

"That's right. And make it while you were sleeping and sitting in class and eating lunch."

"Amazing," Lisa said.

"And if we could have that many hits every day in a year, we'd all earn close to four thousand dollars each," Nevin said.

"That's even more amazing," Lisa said, as we all started counting and spending the money in our heads. Making money would make my father happy and let him know that skating could be serious.

"But the hard part isn't getting them to look for a day but to keep them looking, day after day after day," Nevin said.

He was right. I felt deflated, and then I remembered what Bam Bam had said. The secret was to keep putting on new stuff.

"If we update regularly, people will come back to check on it regularly," I said.

"Exactly," Nevin agreed. "And our sponsor — and they are our sponsor if you all agree — they said they had some ideas on how we could do that."

"What sort of ideas?" Wally asked.

"They didn't say, but I'm sure they'll be good. First things first, though," Nevin said. "If we agree to their sponsorship, I'll put the ad up and make the link right away so we don't lose any more money. Each of those hits you see is free right now."

The hit wheel continued to click up.

"Do it," I said, "and do it now."

"Yeah, hurry," Wally agreed.

"Me too," Lisa echoed. "The sooner the better."

"I hoped you'd all agree. You head off for class and I'll take care of everything. And remember, as you're sitting there you'll actually be earning money at the same time."

Chapter Twelve

"It's definitely started to go down," Nevin said.

"How many hits have we had altogether?" Wally asked.

"In the past week we've had over ninety thousand hits."

"And since we've been getting paid for the last eighty thousand at a cent a hit, that means that we've made over eight hundred dollars, or two hundred bucks each," I said.

"But the rate of hits has been declining. We only had four thousand visits today. Our peak was four days ago, and it's been going down each and every day," Nevin said.

"But we've been adding new material," Wally said.

"Obviously not good new material," Nevin said. "We have to upload something that people will want to see."

"I've been thinking about some tricks," I said.

"Tricks are good, but I've been looking at the comments in our guest book and talking to our sponsor and it seems pretty clear what the webcrawlers want," Nevin said.

"What?" I asked.

"For starters, the most popular video clip we have is the one where you're running up and over the security car," he answered.

"So you want me run up another security car?"

"No, of course not. You've already done that. I was thinking more of a police car."

"You're joking, right?"

He shook his head. "I'm serious."

"You're seriously *crazy* if you think I'm going to run over a police car and be chased by some cops. Real cops are different than rent-a-cops."

"I didn't say anything about being chased by anybody," Nevin said. "We'll find an empty police car and you can skate up to it and then run over top."

"And just where do you think we're going to find an empty police car?" I asked.

Nevin shrugged. "I thought we'd hang around a donut shop and wait for them to go inside. The whole thing shouldn't take more than a few seconds if you think about it."

Part of me thought he was crazy. The other part knew that I was crazy enough to be excited about giving it a shot.

"What about us?" Wally asked.

"It looks like the people visiting the page want to see more of Lisa," Nevin said.

"I can do some more tricks," she said.

"That isn't necessarily what they mean. They want to see more of you. More close-up pictures, maybe less clothing, no helmet."

"Hold on," I said, "we're not putting Lisa in a bikini to satisfy some perverts."

"Nobody's talking about a bikini — although that would attract more hits. We could use your school pictures, or just some shots of you sitting around or talking or standing on your board."

"I guess that would be okay," Lisa said.

She wasn't arguing the way I thought she would. Maybe she liked the idea. I knew I certainly didn't like some of the comments people had been posting in our guest book. Lisa was really good-looking, but it wasn't helping me any for kids around the world to be telling her that.

"And me?" Wally asked.

"More tricks," Nevin said. "If you're Wally the Wall, they want you to do some more aerial stunts, climbing the wall, riding the rail."

"The sort of trick you've almost been hitting for the past four months," I said. "You can do it."

"And you should all be riding the new boards."

We'd gotten the new boards from Street Illegal. They were nice boards, flashy, good graphics, nice handling.

"So when do we go out and tape?" Wally asked.

"Sooner is better. How about right after school?" I asked.

All three nodded. "Good. See you all at the Super Save at around four thirty."

"How about if we go to a donut shop first?" Wally suggested.

"We can get food after," I said.

"I wasn't talking about food. I thought we'd go looking for a police car."

"Tell you what. You land that jump of yours and then we'll find a police car and I'll give it a shot," I said. "Deal?"

"Deal," Wally agreed.

We stood, boards in hand — new Street Illegal boards — waiting for Nevin to set up. There was no point in hitting a trick unless it was being taped. Nevin gave us the thumbs-up.

"Okay, Wally, go for it."

He didn't move. It was like he hadn't heard me.

"Come on, we don't have much time. I really don't want to be here if security arrives."

"Could make for some interesting shots if they do," Lisa said.

"That's what I'm afraid of. Shots to the side of my head as they break my new board over my old skull."

Lisa laughed. She'd been easing up on me over the past week…maybe this was going to work out okay.

Wally hadn't laughed — or blinked. He looked frozen.

"You can do it, Wally," I said. "All you need is a little more speed. Go higher up the bank, okay?"

Wally nodded.

"Remember, no guts, no glory. No pain, no gain. Go big or go home."

"And going home is okay," Lisa said. "You don't have to do this if you don't want to."

"It's okay," Wally said. "I'll do it. I *want* to do it."

"That's the way," I said, although, looking at him, it was obvious he wasn't feeling good about it.

"I can make the trick," Wally said.

"I know you can do it," I said, offering encouragement.

Wally gave a timid little smile, nodded and started away for the bank.

"Do you really think he can do it?" Lisa asked quietly.

"He's a good skater. Besides, sometimes you have to just go for it regardless of what happens."

"And sometimes you don't," Lisa said. I knew she wasn't just talking about Wally and the jump.

I turned away from her. Wally was by the bank. He skated up high — higher than I'd ever seen him before. He did a kick flip and started back down, picking up more and more speed — he was flying! He kicked hard and the board jumped up onto the rail. He went grinding along the top ... suddenly the board got caught and Wally went flying through the air, crashing into the pavement!

He landed and his head bounced against the asphalt with a sickening thud. Then the only sound was the wheels of his board as it went skittering away.

"Wally!" Lisa screamed.

Her cry unfroze me. I raced to Wally's side. There was a gash on the side of his head and blood was forming a puddle beneath him. His right leg was sticking out at a strange angle. His eyes were closed — he was knocked out! His chest heaved and I heard him inhale. He was breathing!

"Call an ambulance!" I gasped. "Somebody call an ambulance!"

Chapter Thirteen

"Phillip?"

I was almost asleep. The voice made me jump. Wally's mother stood in front of me.

"You've been here all night?" she asked in her heavy Polish accent.

I nodded. I'd spent the night in the little waiting area down the hall from Wally's hospital room. My parents had tried to convince me to go home, but when I refused to leave they reluctantly let me stay.

"You *good* friend to Wally," she said. "*First* friend in new country still *best* friend."

Another wave of guilt hit me. A good friend would have stopped him instead of pushing him.

"How is he doing?"

"Sleeping. Groggy because of all the drugs given for his pain in leg."

I knew Wally was hurting. Just before the ambulance had arrived he'd regained consciousness and begun howling in pain. Wally was one of the toughest people I'd ever known, so I could only imagine how bad the pain must have been. Actually, I didn't want to imagine.

"I know his leg is broken. How bad is it?"

"Need operation to put in pin, but first swelling must go down. Probably tomorrow will do surgery."

"Wally is tough. He'll get better fast."

Mrs. Waltniski bent down and kissed me on the forehead. "Good boy, good kind boy."

I felt like arguing. I wasn't that good or kind. I liked things to go my way. Now Wally, he *was* good and kind.

"I go home," she said. "Wally asleep and have to get other kids ready for school. Do you want ride?"

I shook my head. "I'd like to stay here. Do you think I could sit in Wally's room? I'd be quiet. I wouldn't wake him."

"Go, keep him company. Good that somebody will be with him. If he wakes, tell him that his daddy will be coming soon."

"I'll tell him." I stood up and Mrs. Waltniski threw her arms around me and gave me a hug. I felt my rib cage compress as she squeezed. Everybody in the family was strong. She released her grip and walked away, leaving me in the waiting area.

Now that I could go and see Wally, I didn't know if I wanted to. It would be easier to sit here and read fifteen-year-old copies of *National Geographic*. But I couldn't do that.

I walked down the hall until I reached Wally's room. I peeked in the door. There were two beds — one empty; the other holding Wally. He was all tucked in, his eyes closed. He looked peaceful, like he was sleeping.

I tiptoed into the room and slowly lowered myself into the chair beside the bed. There was a low whistling sound — Wally breathing through his nose. The chair was soft and I was so tired. Maybe if I closed my eyes I could get a little more sleep. If I went to sleep, maybe I could wake up and this would all be a bad dream.

"Phil?"

My eyes popped open. Wally was looking at me.

"It's good to see you," he said.

"It's better to see you. How are you feeling?"

"Tired … sore … doped up like I'm floating on a cloud."

"I just wanted to tell you I'm so sorry," I said. "It's all my fault."

"Your fault? You didn't miss the jump," Wally said.

"But you only did it because I pushed you."

"I did it because I wanted to do it. You had faith in me, that's all. It's good to have people believe in you," Wally said. "Maybe I should apologize to you and Lisa and Nevin for blowing the trick." Wally paused. "Did Nevin get it all on tape?"

I nodded.

"Have you seen it?"

I nodded again, fighting the urge to shudder. It was even worse seeing it replayed, especially in slow motion.

"I hope he brings it in so I can see it."

"You want to see it?" I couldn't believe it.

"Why not? I can't really remember it and I'd like to see the footage before Nevin posts it on the site."

"He's not going to post it," I said.

"Why not?" Wally asked. "A good slam is just as interesting to watch as a good trick. It was a good slam wasn't it?"

"One of the best I've ever seen," I admitted.

"Good, because that's the last thing of mine that will ever be posted. I'm retiring."

"You're going to stop skating?"

"This leg isn't going to give me much choice. I'll be in a cast for at least two months."

"You can skate after that," I said.

"My mother may have some other ideas."

"Maybe I should stop skating for a while too," I suggested.

"Yeah, right, like that's going to happen," he laughed.

"Seriously, maybe I shouldn't skate for a while."

"You can't quit right now. You still have one more trick you have to do," Wally said.

"What trick?"

"Are you forgetting our deal? I tried my trick so you have to jump the police car."

"You're joking, right?"

He shook his head. "A deal is a deal. Make sure Nevin tapes it so I can see it. Who knows, if things go wrong, you and I might become roommates. There is an empty bed," he said, motioning to the bed beside him.

"Thanks for the offer."

"I think it might be good if I went back to sleep now," Wally said. His eyes were already closed.

"That's a good idea. I'll just stay, if you don't mind. Your dad is coming in a while and I'll wait until he gets here."

"Sure," Wally said. "When you go, could you do me a favor?"

"Of course, just name it."

"Find Lisa. Tell her you were an idiot for what you did and that you're sorry."

"I already told her that."

"Then tell her again. This time make sure you tell her what a jerk you were."

"Thanks."

"It's the truth," Wally said.

"I know," I admitted.

"And just keep telling her that until she finally agrees to go out with you again just to shut you up. Can you do that?"

"I don't know if it'll work."

"Maybe it will, and maybe it won't, but you have to try. As a wise man once said to me, no guts, no glory, and I've certainly spilled enough guts to prove it."

"Wally, I'm so sorry and—"

"Shut up already. Now leave me alone so I can sleep."

"I'll just wait until your father gets here."

"Go now. Go and talk to Lisa. I'm giving you a head start."

"A head start?" I asked.

"Maybe it's the drugs talking, but I've been thinking. Once I'm out of this bed, if you're not already with Lisa again, I'm asking her out."

"You're not joking, are you," I said.

He shook his head. "Sometimes you just have to go for it…no matter what happens. Right?"

I stood up. "You get back to sleep and I'll go and talk to Lisa. Thanks for the advice… and the head start."

"That's what friends are for. Especially best friends," he said, his words hardly a whisper, his eyes closed.

I had the urge to bend down and give him a hug or even a kiss on the forehead, like his mother had given me, but that was way too goofy.

"Later, Wally," I said.

"Later…and say hello to Lisa for me," he said, the last words fading to nothing.

I stopped at the door. It looked like he was already asleep. "Thanks, Wally."

He was right. Sometimes you have to go

for it. And sometimes you don't. The hard part was deciding which was which. This time I knew.

I was going over to Lisa's house and I was going to apologize again. And again and again if I needed to. I just hoped she'd listen.

But I had one more thing to do first. I had to find Nevin. And an empty police car.

Also by Eric Walters

Overdrive

"Go! Get out of here!"

I saw red flashing lights behind me in the distance. For a split second I took my foot off the accelerator. Then I pressed down harder and took a quick left turn.

Jake has finally got his driver's license, and tonight he has his brother's car as well. He and his friend Mickey take the car out and cruise the strip. When they challenge another driver to a road race, a disastrous chain reaction causes an accident. Jake and Mickey leave the scene, trying to convince themselves they were not involved. The driver of the other car was Luke, a one-time friend of Jake's. Jake struggles to choose the right thing to do. Should he pretend he was not involved and hope Luke doesn't remember? Or should he go to the police?

OTHER TITLES IN THE ORCA SOUNDINGS SERIES

NEW
Orca Soundings novel

No More Pranks
by Monique Polak

The noise — it sounded now like a loud bleating sound — was coming from the water. As I turned to look in the direction of the Saguenay, I saw something huge and black. Against the dark horizon it looked as big as a mountain. But something told me it was a whale. Something else told me he was in trouble — big trouble.

Suspended from school for pulling pranks, Pete is sent to spend the summer working with his uncle, a whale-watching guide in a tourist town far from the city.

Unable to give up on practical jokes completely, Pete learns about whales and helps lead tours. When a whale is injured by a reckless tour guide, Pete struggles to save the animal. Then Pete has to pull the most important prank of his life to bring the guide to justice.

NEW
Orca Soundings novel

Charmed
by Carrie Mac

Cody Dillon comes and rescues me (RESCUES ME!). He takes me to his apartment (HIS OWN APARTMENT!) and runs me a bubble bath. He lights a bunch of candles and turns the light off. He sits on the floor and keeps me company. He says I can stay here as long as I want. Um, hello, heaven? Izzy McAfferty has arrived, in case anyone wants to know.

Izzy's mother works far away and leaves Izzy at home, alone with Rob the Slob. Angry at her mother and trying to deal with school, friends and the attentions of charismatic Cody Dillon, Izzy finds her life swirling out of control. After "borrowing" money from her mother's boyfriend, she is forced to leave home until she can repay it. Ending up with Cody and living in the city, Izzy makes misguided choices that are all wrong.

NEW
Orca Soundings novel

My Time as Caz Hazard
by Tanya Lloyd Kyi

"How can you be like this? What if this was our fault?" I could feel my voice growing loud and shrill.

"Shut up!" Amanda grabbed my arm, hard. "You're not making sense. What did we have to do with it? No one kills herself over a ripped shirt. Understand?"

Moving to a new school, Caz is told she is dyslexic and sent to Special Education classes. She tries to fit in and get by while suffering the taunts and abuse that others throw at the students in her class. Her friendship with Amanda leads her into new territory — shoplifting and skipping school. Coupled with her parents' impending separation, her life is anything but stable and continues to spiral out of control. And when Caz and Amanda's behavior seems to contribute to a classmate's suicide, Caz must take a long hard look at her life.